VISHWAM...

ONCE, LONG AGO, WHILE ROAMING OVER THE EARTH WITH HIS HUNDRED SONS AND VAST ARMIES, THE MIGHTY KING VISHWAMITRA CAME UPON THE HERMITAGE OF THE POWERFUL SAGE VASISHTHA.

IT IS SURPRISING, BUT THE SIGHT OF THESE ASCETICS WHO HAVE RENOUNCED THE WORLD EXHILARATES ME.

VISHWAMITRA WALKED UP TO VASISHTHA.

I BOW MY HEAD AT YOUR FEET.

WELCOME O KING. COME, SIT DOWN. I PRESUME ALL IS WELL IN YOUR KINGDOM.

VISHWAMITRA SAT NEAR THE SAGE AND THEY TALKED OF MANY THINGS. THEN —

I WISH TO HONOUR YOU AND YOUR ROYAL RETINUE. PLEASE LET ME BE THE HOST AT A BANQUET WORTHY OF YOU.

O WISE SAGE, THE VERY SIGHT OF YOU IS A PRIVILEGE AND THIS GRACIOUS WELCOME, AN HONOUR. PRAY PERMIT US TO DEPART NOW.

I INSIST THAT YOU BE THE GUESTS AT MY FEAST.

WE WILL STAY, SINCE IT IS YOUR WISH.

THEREUPON VASISHTHA SENT FOR HIS FAVOURITE COW, THE DIVINE KAMADHENU.*

DEAR KAMADHENU, PROVIDE US WITH FOOD FIT FOR A GREAT KING.

* THE WISH - FULFILLING

IN AN INSTANT, THERE EMERGED FROM THE DIVINE COW, CHOICE FOOD FOR THE ROYAL VISITORS.

VISHWAMITRA AND HIS MEN ATE TO THEIR HEART'S CONTENT.

I HAVE NEVER TASTED SUCH DELICACIES BEFORE. KAMADHENU SHOULD BELONG TO ME!

WHEN THE FEAST WAS OVER —

KAMADHENU IS A JEWEL AND JEWELS BELONG TO THE KING. BY RIGHT SHE SHOULD BE MINE. YET I WILL GIVE YOU A HUNDRED THOUSAND MILCH COWS IN RETURN.

NO. I CANNOT PART WITH HER EVEN FOR 1,00,00,000 COWS.

VASISHTHA'S REFUSAL MADE VISHWAMITRA'S DESIRE KEENER. HE INCREASED HIS PRICE.

I WILL GIVE YOU 14,000 ELEPHANTS HARNESSED AND CAPARISONED IN GOLD, 800 CHARIOTS OF SOLID GOLD EACH DRAWN BY FOUR MILK-WHITE HORSES, 11,000 THOROUGHBRED HORSES ALSO HARNESSED IN GOLD AND 10 MILLION COWS OF VARIOUS HUES. ALL THIS AND AS MUCH GOLD AS YOU WANT, SHALL BE YOURS. GIVE ME KAMADHENU.

BUT VASISHTHA TURNED DOWN THE OFFER.

FOR NO TREASURE ON EARTH WILL I PART WITH HER, O KING. SHE IS THE VERY SOURCE OF MY SPIRITUAL LIFE. SHE PROVIDES ME WITH ALL I NEED FOR MY RITUALS.

THEN I SHALL HAVE TO TAKE HER AWAY BY FORCE.

VISHWAMITRA CALLED TO HIS MEN.

SEIZE THE SAGE'S COW OF PLENTY AND BRING HER TO ME.

THE KING'S MEN FELL UPON THE BEWILDERED KAMADHENU.

WHY DOES THE HOLY ONE PERMIT THIS OUTRAGE? I HAVE ALWAYS LOVED AND SERVED HIM!! I WILL SHAKE OFF MY TORMENTORS AND GO TO HIM.

KAMADHENU TOSSED ASIDE HER CAPTORS...

...AND FLED.

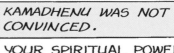

SHE STOOD BEFORE VASISHTHA, WEEPING AND LOWING.

O LORD, HAVE YOU FORSAKEN ME? DID YOU NOT SEE HOW I WAS TREATED?

DEAR ONE, I AM HELPLESS AGAINST THE KING AND HIS MIGHTY ARMY.

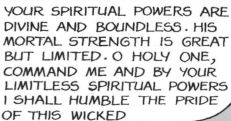

KAMADHENU WAS NOT CONVINCED.

YOUR SPIRITUAL POWERS ARE DIVINE AND BOUNDLESS. HIS MORTAL STRENGTH IS GREAT BUT LIMITED. O HOLY ONE, COMMAND ME AND BY YOUR LIMITLESS SPIRITUAL POWERS I SHALL HUMBLE THE PRIDE OF THIS WICKED WARRIOR.

SO BE IT, KAMADHENU.

SO KAMADHENU LOWED LOUD AND LONG. HORDES AND HORDES OF WARRIORS SPRANG UP MIRACULOUSLY AND CHARGED AT THE KING'S SOLDIERS...

...AND SOON DESTROYED THEM.

ENRAGED, THE SONS OF VISHWAMITRA RUSHED TOWARDS VASISHTHA.

THE SAGE STOOD FIRM AND CALM. HE UTTERED BUT ONE SYLLABLE...

HMM..M.M

...THE MERE SOUND OF WHICH BURNT THE PRINCES AND THEIR HORSES, CHARIOTS, WEAPONS AND ALL.

NOW I HAVE BUT THE ONE SON WHO STAYED BACK TO RULE THE KINGDOM.

VISHWAMITRA RETURNED TO HIS KINGDOM FULL OF GRIEF AND SHAME. THERE —

MY SON, THE KINGDOM IS YOURS. RULE VIRTU-OUSLY OVER IT. I PLAN TO RETIRE TO THE FORESTS FOR A WHILE.

HE WENT STRAIGHT TO THE HIMALAYAS AND BEGAN PRACTIS-ING SEVERE AUSTERITIES

I SHALL PROPI-TIATE LORD SHIVA AND BY HIS GRACE AVENGE THE DEATH OF MY GLORIOUS SONS.

AT LAST SHIVA WAS PLEASED. HE STOOD BEFORE VISHWAMITRA.

THE BOON THAT YOU SEEK O KING, SHALL BE YOURS.

BY YOUR GRACE, LET ALL KNOWLEDGE OF WEAPONS AND WARFARE BE MINE.

SHIVA GRANTED THE BOON AND WENT BACK TO HIS ABODE.

A TRIUMPHANT VISHWAMITRA NOW TURNED HIS FOOTSTEPS TOWARDS VASISHTHA'S HERMITAGE.

MERCY, O KING. MERCY.

AS SOON AS VISHWAMITRA REACHED THE HERMITAGE HE SENT OUT FLAMING MISSILES AND SET IT ABLAZE.

RUN!

RUN!

THIS HERMITAGE IS NO LONGER A HAVEN FOR THE HOLY.

VASISHTHA TRIED TO STOP THEM, BUT IN VAIN.

WAIT. DO NOT RUN AWAY. I WILL DESTROY THE EVIL KING.

A DEADLY SILENCE DESCENDED OVER THE DESERTED HERMITAGE. IT WAS BROKEN BY THE RESONANT VOICE OF VASISHTHA.

WICKED, DELUDED ONE. YOU HAVE WANTONLY DESTROYED MY ANCIENT HERMITAGE. FOR THIS YOU SHALL DIE.

SNATCHING HIS STAFF HE ADVANCED TOWARDS VISHWAMITRA.

BEWARE! MY WEAPONS WILL CONSUME YOU.

EVIL WARRIOR, LET US SEE HOW YOUR WEAPONS OF DESTRUCTION ENCOUNTER SPIRITUAL POWER.

VISHWAMITRA HURLED THE WEAPON. BUT —

ADMIT NOW, THE IMPOTENCE OF ALL YOUR WEAPONS.

VISHWAMITRA IN DESPERATION HURLED WEAPON, AFTER...

...WEAPON.

BUT THEY WERE ALL ABSORBED BY VASISHTHA'S STAFF.

AT LAST VISHWAMITRA SENT OUT THE FATAL BRAHMASTRA. BUT...

...VASISHTHA SUBDUED EVEN THAT.

VISHWAMITRA, HIS PRIDE HUMBLED, HAD TO ADMIT DEFEAT.

THE MIGHT OF A WARRIOR IS USELESS. SPIRITUAL POWER IS THE GREATEST POWER OF ALL. I SHALL REALISE BRAHMAN AND THE STATUS OF BRAHMARSHI.*

HE LAID DOWN HIS ARMS AND WENT HOME TO HIS QUEEN.

I WANT TO BECOME A BRAHMARSHI. WE SHALL GO TO A HERMITAGE IN THE SOUTH. THERE YOU WILL HELP ME IN MY PENANCES.

AS YOU COMMAND, MY LORD.

SO VISHWAMITRA AND HIS QUEEN SET OUT. THEY REACHED THE CHOSEN HERMITAGE AND...

THIS TIME I SHALL SEEK THE FAVOUR OF BRAHMA.

...VISHWAMITRA BEGAN HIS PENANCES. IN THAT PERIOD FOUR VIRTUOUS AND MIGHTY SONS WERE BORN TO HIM.

* BRAHMA RISHI.

THEN VISHWAMITRA CONTINUED HIS AUSTERITIES WITH GREATER SEVERITY UNTIL BRAHMA HAD TO APPEAR BEFORE HIM.

YOU ARE THE GREATEST ASCETIC AMONG KINGS. I CONFER UPON YOU THE STATUS OF RAJARSHI.*

THE STATUS OF MERE RAJARSHI IS NO REWARD FOR THE PENANCES I HAVE UNDERGONE. I SHALL ASK FOR...

BUT BRAHMA HAD ALREADY DEPARTED. VISHWAMITRA WAS DEJECTED.

IN SPITE OF ALL MY PENANCES I AM ONLY A RAJARSHI TO THE GODS. I WILL STRIVE HARDER FOR GREATER SPIRITUAL POWERS.

MEANWHILE TRISHANKU, A GREAT KING OF THOSE TIMES, WAS SUDDENLY SEIZED WITH AN AMBITION.

I WILL ENTER HEAVEN IN MY MORTAL BODY. I SHALL ASK MY GURU, VASISHTHA, TO HELP ME PERFORM A SACRIFICE TO ACHIEVE THIS.

HE SENT FOR VASISHTHA.

I WISH TO ENTER HEAVEN IN THIS MORTAL FRAME OF MINE, SO...

NO! O KING! THAT CAN NEVER BE!

* RAJA RISHI

BUT TRISHANKU REFUSED TO GIVE UP THE IDEA.

IF MY GURU WILL NOT HELP ME, HIS SONS WILL. I SHALL GO TO THEIR HERMITAGE IN THE SOUTH.

THERE TRISHANKU TOLD THE SONS OF VASISHTHA OF THEIR FATHER'S DECISION.

PRAY, WILL YOU BECOME MY GURUS AND HELP ME?

HOW DARE YOU SEEK OUR AID WHEN YOUR GURU, OUR WISE FATHER, HAS DISAPPROVED. YOU ARE NOT FIT TO CLAIM HIM AS YOUR GURU, YOU IGNORANT ONE.

BUT TRISHANKU WAS BENT UPON PERFORMING THE SACRIFICE.

THEN I SHALL HAVE TO SEEK THE HELP OF SOME OTHER SAGE.

THE SONS OF VASISHTHA WERE FURIOUS WITH THE ADAMANT KING.

O EVIL KING, MAY YOU BECOME A CHANDALA*.

TO HIS DISMAY TRISHANKU FOUND HIS BODY TRANSFORMED.

ALAS! ALAS! WHAT HAVE I, A VIRTUOUS KING, DONE TO DESERVE THIS? WHICH SAGE WILL HELP ME NOW, OUTCASTE AS I AM?

THEN SUDDENLY, HE REMEMBERED VISHWAMITRA.

I WILL GO TO THE RAJARSHI. HE WILL HELP ME.

AS HE EXPECTED, VISHWAMITRA RECEIVED HIM COMPASSIONATELY AND LISTENED TO HIS TALE OF WOE.

O HOLY SAGE, APART FROM YOU THERE IS NONE I CAN TURN TO. I BESEECH YOU, HELP ME OUT OF THIS PLIGHT.

* AN OUTCASTE

VISHWAMITRA CONSOLED AND COMFORTED THE MISERABLE KING.

YOU ARE A VIRTUOUS PERSON. I WILL HELP YOU PERFORM THE SACRIFICE. YOU WILL ENTER HEAVEN AND IN THIS VERY FORM WHICH YOUR GURU'S SONS HAVE IMPOSED ON YOU.

VISHWAMITRA SUMMONED HIS SONS TO HIM.

MAKE ALL ARRANGEMENTS FOR THE SACRIFICE.

NEXT VISHWAMITRA CALLED HIS DISCIPLES TO HIM.

INVITE ALL THE PIOUS AND THE LEARNED OF THE LAND HERE FOR THE GREAT SACRI-FICE.

THE DISCIPLES RETURNED AFTER A FEW DAYS.

SAGE VASISHTHA AND HIS SONS REFUSE TO COME. THE SONS SAY THEY WOULD BE DEFILED.*

MAY THEY BE DESTROYED FOR DISREGARDING ONE WHO IS A SAGE AND FREE OF GUILT.

* ASSOCIATING ONESELF WITH UNTOUCHABLES MADE ONE UNCLEAN.

WHEN THOSE WHO HAD ACCEPTED THE INVITATION ASSEMBLED—

THIS VIRTUOUS KING SEEKS YOUR GOODWILL FOR THIS SACRIFICE IN A NOBLE PURSUIT.

THEN THE RITES BEGAN, WITH VISHWAMITRA OFFICIATING AS THE CHIEF PRIEST.

WHEN THE RITES WERE OVER—

O DEVAS*, COME YE FROM THE HEAVENS. ACCEPT THESE OFFERINGS AND LEAD THIS GREAT KING TO HEAVEN IN HIS OWN BODY.

VISHWAMITRA WAITED. BUT NONE OF THE DEVAS APPEARED. HE WAS ENRAGED.

O KING, I WILL RAISE YOU TO HEAVEN ON THE STRENGTH OF ALL THE SPIRITUAL POWERS I HAVE ACCUMULATED.

VISHWAMITRA THEN LOOKED SKYWARDS.

MAY YOU ASCEND TO HEAVEN AS YOU ARE, O VIRTUOUS KING.

* GODS

17

HARDLY HAD VISHWAMITRA UTTERED THESE WORDS THAN THE ASCENSION OF TRISHANKU BEGAN.

BUT WHEN HE REACHED HEAVEN, INDRA AND THE DEVAS BARRED HIS ENTRY.

WRETCH! YOU HAVE BEEN CURSED BY YOUR GURU'S SONS. HEAVEN HAS NO PLACE FOR YOU. MAY YOU GO DOWN TO THE DEPTHS OF THE EARTH.

TRISHANKU BEGAN FALLING DOWN, DOWN—

SAVE ME! O HOLY ONE, SAVE ME!

VISHWAMITRA WOULD NOT ACCEPT DEFEAT.

MAY YOU STOP WHERE YOU ARE. I SHALL CREATE A HEAVEN AROUND YOU.

AND VISHWAMITRA CREATED SEVEN PLANETS, THE SAPTARSHIS* AND TWENTY-SEVEN STARS. BUT HE WAS NOT SATISFIED.

I WILL CREATE ANOTHER INDRA. OR BETTER STILL I WILL HURL INDRA OUT OF HEAVEN AND MAKE TRISHANKU THE KING OF THE DEVAS!

WHEN THE DEVAS DIVINED HIS INTENTIONS, THEY WERE PERTURBED.

WE MUST STOP HIM.

THEY APPEARED BEFORE HIM AND PLEADED WITH HIM.

O SAGE, THE KING HAS BEEN CURSED BY HIS GURU'S SONS. HOW CAN WE GIVE HIM A PLACE IN HEAVEN?

* SAPTA RISHI

BUT VISHWAMITRA WAS FIRM.

I HAVE PROMISED TO HELP HIM. LET HIM ENTER YOUR HEAVEN. LET THE PLANETS I HAVE CREATED EXIST AS LONG AS YOUR HEAVEN DOES. THEN INDRA SHALL REMAIN IN HEAVEN, THE SOLE KING OF THE DEVAS.

SO BE IT. TRISHANKU, SURROUNDED BY THE PLANETS THAT SHINE ON HIM, SHALL BECOME IMMORTAL AND REMAIN SUSPENDED IN HEAVEN, HEAD DOWNWARDS.

AS THE DEVAS, HEAVING SIGHS OF RELIEF, DEPARTED TO HEAVEN—

EVEN AS A RAJARSHI, VISHWAMITRA HAS HUMBLED US. WE MUST ENSURE THAT HE NEVER BECOMES A BRAHMARSHI.

I HAVE HUMBLED THE DEVAS BUT EXHAUSTED MY SPIRITUAL POWERS. I WILL START ALL OVER AGAIN.

HE TURNED TO HIS SONS AND DISCIPLES.

THE WORLD HAS BEEN TOO MUCH WITH ME HERE. MY PENANCES HAVE COME TO NAUGHT. I SHALL GO WEST TO THE PEACEFUL PUSHKAR TO RESUME MY PENANCES.

MEANWHILE AMBARISHA, KING OF AYODHYA, HAD DECIDED TO PERFORM A SACRIFICE. BUT —

YOUR MAJESTY, THE SACRIFICIAL ANIMAL HAS BEEN STOLEN.

AMBARISHA HUNTED FAR AND WIDE FOR THE ANIMAL. BUT AS INDRA WAS THE UNKNOWN THIEF HIS SEARCH WAS HOPELESS.

THE PRIEST GAVE HIM THE ONLY ALTERNATIVE.

YOU WILL HAVE TO PROVIDE A HUMAN VICTIM TO COMPLETE THE SACRIFICE. OR ELSE GREAT HARM WILL BEFALL YOUR KINGDOM AND YOUR SUBJECTS.

AMBARISHA SET OUT AGAIN. HIS QUEST TOOK HIM THROUGH CITIES AND FORESTS TILL HE CAME UPON THE HERMITAGE WHERE RICHIKA LIVED WITH HIS WIFE AND SONS.

GREAT KING, WHAT BRINGS YOU TO OUR HUMBLE ABODE?

AMBARISHA TOLD HIM ALL.

O SAGE, GIVE ME ONE OF YOUR SONS FOR 100,000 COWS AND HELP ME COMPLETE THE SACRIFICE.

RICHIKA AND HIS WIFE LOOKED AT EACH OTHER.

I WILL NEVER GIVE UP MY ELDEST SON.

MY YOUNGEST SHALL EVER REMAIN WITH US.

SHUNAHSHEPA, THE MIDDLE SON, STEPPED FORWARD BEFORE HIS PARENTS COULD SAY MORE.

TAKE ME, THE MIDDLE SON, O KING, AND GIVE MY PARENTS 100,000 COWS.

DELIGHTED THAT HIS SEARCH HAD COME TO AN END, AMBARISHA TOOK SHUNAHSHEPA AND MOUNTING HIS CHARIOT TURNED HOMEWARD.

ON THE WAY THEY HAD TO PASS THROUGH THE FOREST OF PUSHKARA.

LET US REST FOR A WHILE AT THAT HERMITAGE OVER THERE.

AS THE KING RESTED, SHUNAHSHEPA WANDERED ABOUT THE HERMITAGE. SUDDENLY –

SAGE VISHWAMITRA, MY MOTHER'S BROTHER HERE!

SHUNAHSHEPA RAN TO HIM, FELL AT HIS FEET AND TOLD HIM ALL. THEN –

O HOLY ONE, I HAVE NEITHER FATHER NOR MOTHER. O LORD, PROTECT ME. LET ME LIVE, LEAD A SPIRITUAL LIFE AND ATTAIN HEAVEN.

BE CONSOLED, O VIRTUOUS SON. I WILL NOT LET YOU DIE.

VISHWAMITRA TURNED TO HIS SONS.

SHUNAHSHEPA HAS SOUGHT MY PROTECTION. ONE OF YOU TAKE HIS PLACE AND RESCUE HIM. I HAVE GIVEN HIM MY WORD. HELP ME KEEP IT.

O FATHER, WOULD YOU ABANDON ONE OF YOUR OWN SONS TO PROTECT ANOTHER'S?

YOU ARROGANT SONS. HAVE YOU NO AFFECTION FOR ME? MAY YOU LOSE YOUR CASTE AND WANDER ABOUT THE EARTH EATING THE FLESH OF DOGS.

VISHWAMITRA THEN ADDRESSED SHUNAHSHEPA.

I WILL TEACH YOU TWO MANTRAS IN PRAISE OF INDRA. REPEAT THEM AT THE SACRIFICIAL ALTAR AND YOU WILL BE SAVED.

SHUNAHSHEPA LEARNT THE MANTRAS AND RETURNED TO AMBARISHA.

O KING, LET US HASTEN TO THE SACRIFICIAL GROUND.

WHEN THEY REACHED THE SACRIFICIAL ALTAR, AMBARISHA HANDED SHUNAHSHEPA OVER TO THE PRIEST.

SHUNAHSHEPA REPEATED THE MANTRAS THAT VISHWAMITRA HAD TAUGHT HIM. SUDDENLY INDRA APPEARED BEFORE HIM.

I AM PLEASED WITH YOUR WORSHIP. MAY THE LONG LIFE YOU SEEK BE YOURS.

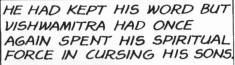

HE HAD KEPT HIS WORD BUT VISHWAMITRA HAD ONCE AGAIN SPENT HIS SPIRITUAL FORCE IN CURSING HIS SONS.

THIS TIME I WILL REMAIN HERE AND RESUME MY PENANCES.

ONE DAY WHILE HE WAS ON THE BANK OF THE PUSHKARA LAKE —

IT'S THE IRRESISTIBLE APSARA, MENAKA. I MUST MAKE HER MINE.

AS MENAKA CAME OUT OF THE LAKE, VISHWAMITRA DECLARED HIS LOVE TO HER.

I AM HONOURED, O VENERABLE SAGE.

A FEW YEARS PASSED BEFORE VISHWAMITRA SUDDENLY REALISED HIS FOLLY.

I SEE NOW! THE DEVAS MUST HAVE SENT YOU HERE TO DISTRACT ME.

MENAKA, AWARE OF THE SAGE'S FIERCE TEMPER, TREMBLED WITH FEAR. BUT THE SAGE WAS KIND TO HER.

GO BACK TO THE DEVAS, O APSARA. MAY YOU FARE WELL.

WHEN MENAKA LEFT —

I SHALL GO TO THE HIMALAYAS AND PERFORM MY PENANCES ON THE BANKS OF THE KAUSHIKI RIVER.

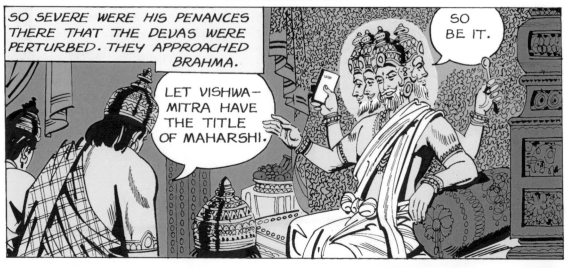

SO SEVERE WERE HIS PENANCES THERE THAT THE DEVAS WERE PERTURBED. THEY APPROACHED BRAHMA.

LET VISHWA-MITRA HAVE THE TITLE OF MAHARSHI.

SO BE IT.

BRAHMA APPEARED BEFORE VISHWAMITRA.

O RISHI, I AM PLEASED WITH YOUR AUSTERITY. YOU HAVE EARNED THE STATUS OF A MAHARSHI.*

MY PENANCES WERE FOR THE STATUS OF A BRAHMARSHI. YOU REGARD ME ONLY AS A MAHARSHI. I WILL HAVE TO SUBDUE MY PASSIONS FURTHER.

YES. YOU HAVE NOT YET GAINED MASTERY OVER YOUR SENSES.

WHEN BRAHMA DEPARTED, VISHWAMITRA INTENSIFIED HIS AUSTERITIES.

IN SUMMER HE STOOD ON ONE FOOT IN THE MIDST OF FIVE BLAZING FIRES, LIVING ONLY ON AIR.

THROUGH THE RAINY SEASON HE CONTINUED STANDING.

AND IN WINTER HE STOOD IN THE MIDDLE OF A COLD STREAM.

THE DEVAS WERE ONCE AGAIN PERTURBED. THEN INDRA HAD AN IDEA.

I WILL ASK THE APSARA RAMBHA OF MY COURT TO DISTRACT HIM.

HE SENT FOR RAMBHA.

YOU MUST ATTRACT MAHARSHI VISHWA-MITRA AND DISTURB HIS PENANCES.

LORD, PLEASE DO NOT SEND ME ON THIS TASK. THE SAGE HAS A TERRIBLE TEMPER AND A READY CURSE.

BUT INDRA REASSURED HER.

DO NOT WORRY, RAMBHA. I WILL TAKE THE FORM OF A CUCKOO AND WILL SIT ON A BRANCH NEAR BY. GO, ADORN YOURSELF.

AS SOON AS RAMBHA WAS READY, THEY CAME TO VISHWAMITRA'S GROVE.

I WILL ROUSE HIM WITH MY NOTES. THAT IS THE MOMENT FOR YOU TO APPROACH HIM.

INDRA BEGAN WARBLING. RAMBHA WALKED TOWARDS VISHWAMITRA.

WHAT HEAVENLY NOTES!

VISHWAMITRA OPENED HIS EYES.

RAMBHA OF INDRA'S COURT? HERE? THIS IS ONE OF INDRA'S TRICKS.

VISHWAMITRA'S RAGE ONCE AGAIN GOT THE BETTER OF HIM.

RAMBHA, FOR THIS IMPERTINENCE MAY YOU BE TURNED INTO ROCK. SO YOU SHALL REMAIN FOR 10,000 YEARS TILL A BRAHMAN COMES AND DELIVERS YOU.

WHEN HE HEARD THIS, INDRA FLED FROM THE SCENE.

ONCE AGAIN MY SPIRITUAL FORCE HAS BEEN CONSUMED BY ANGER. I WILL NEITHER EAT, SPEAK NOR BREATHE TILL I HAVE CONQUERED THIS PASSION.

VISHWAMITRA WENT EASTWARD AND BEGAN HIS MOST SEVERE AUSTERITIES. WHEN HE WAS SURE THAT HE HAD CONQUERED ANGER—

I HAVE SUCCEEDED. I SHALL FIRST BREAK MY LONG FAST.

AS VISHWAMITRA SAT DOWN TO EAT—

O HOLY SAGE, I AM HUNGRY.

IT WAS INDRA WHO HAD COME IN THE GUISE OF A BRAHMAN TO TEST HIM. VISHWAMITRA WITHOUT UTTERING A WORD OFFERED HIM THE FOOD.

AFTER YEARS OF FURTHER PENANCE, THE TERRIBLE POWERS AMASSED BY VISHWAMITRA BEGAN TO EMIT PERVASIVE THICK SMOKE, STRIKING TERROR AMONG THE BEINGS OF THE THREE WORLDS.

TERRIFIED, INDRA AND THE DEVAS WENT TO BRAHMA.

IF THE STATUS OF BRAHMARSHI IS NOT GRANTED TO VISHWAMITRA NOW, HE WILL DESTROY THE THREE WORLDS AND THEN HE WILL BE CONTENT ONLY WITH THE SOVEREIGNTY OF MY HEAVEN.

DO NOT FEAR. I SHALL GRANT HIM THE STATUS OF BRAHMARSHI. HE DESERVES IT.

BRAHMA ACCOMPANIED BY ALL THE DEVAS APPEARED BEFORE THE SAGE.

O VISHWAMITRA, BY THE POWER OF YOUR PENANCES YOU HAVE ACHIEVED THE STATUS OF BRAHMARSHI.

THEN INSTRUCT ME IN THE LORE OF THE BRAHMAN AND LET VASISHTHA ACKNOWLEDGE MY PRESENT STATUS.

THE GODS LED VASISHTHA TO VISHWAMITRA.

MY GREETINGS TO YOU, O BRAHMARSHI.

VISHWAMITRA TOO PAID HOMAGE TO VASISHTHA. THEN, HAVING ACHIEVED WHAT HE HAD SET OUT TO ACHIEVE, VISHWAMITRA ENRICHED THE WORLDS WITH HIS GOOD DEEDS.